MW01632480

Journey to Joy

PRAISE FOR JOURNEY TO JOY

This fairy tale is such good, strong, wise, and delicious medicine! I love the psychologically astute and resonant vibration of it. This is a story for the ages. Of all Christine's works that I absolutely adore, this is now my favorite. All of it makes my heart sing with recognition. The magic of sharing and generosity as greed's transmutation.

–CARMEN ACEVEDO BUTCHER, PhD
Author and Translator of several mystical texts

I absolutely love this fairy tale. It resonated deeply with my own experience of healing, bringing in so many strands such as chronic health issues, the role of animals and nature in recovery, the power of journaling and blessing and many, many more. As a therapist and spiritual accompanier, I will be keeping copies to share with clients and friends.

–POLLY PATON-BROWN, MA
Soul Care Practitioner

This story shares the transformative travels of its heroine, Sophia, and enchants the reader along the way. Populated with healing herbs, wise women and animal allies, we follow Sophia's journey to reclaim a lost part of her soul. Her story reminds us of what is essential to our humanity – the recognition of soul loss and the knowledge of how to retrieve it. In this wonderful fairy tale, the powers of women, nature and kinship weave together, to birth Sophia a-new. We are reminded that if we dare to walk through these life thresholds, we may encounter our demons, yet discover them to be angels on the other side.

– AISLING RICHMOND, MA
Somatic Therapist and Soul Guide

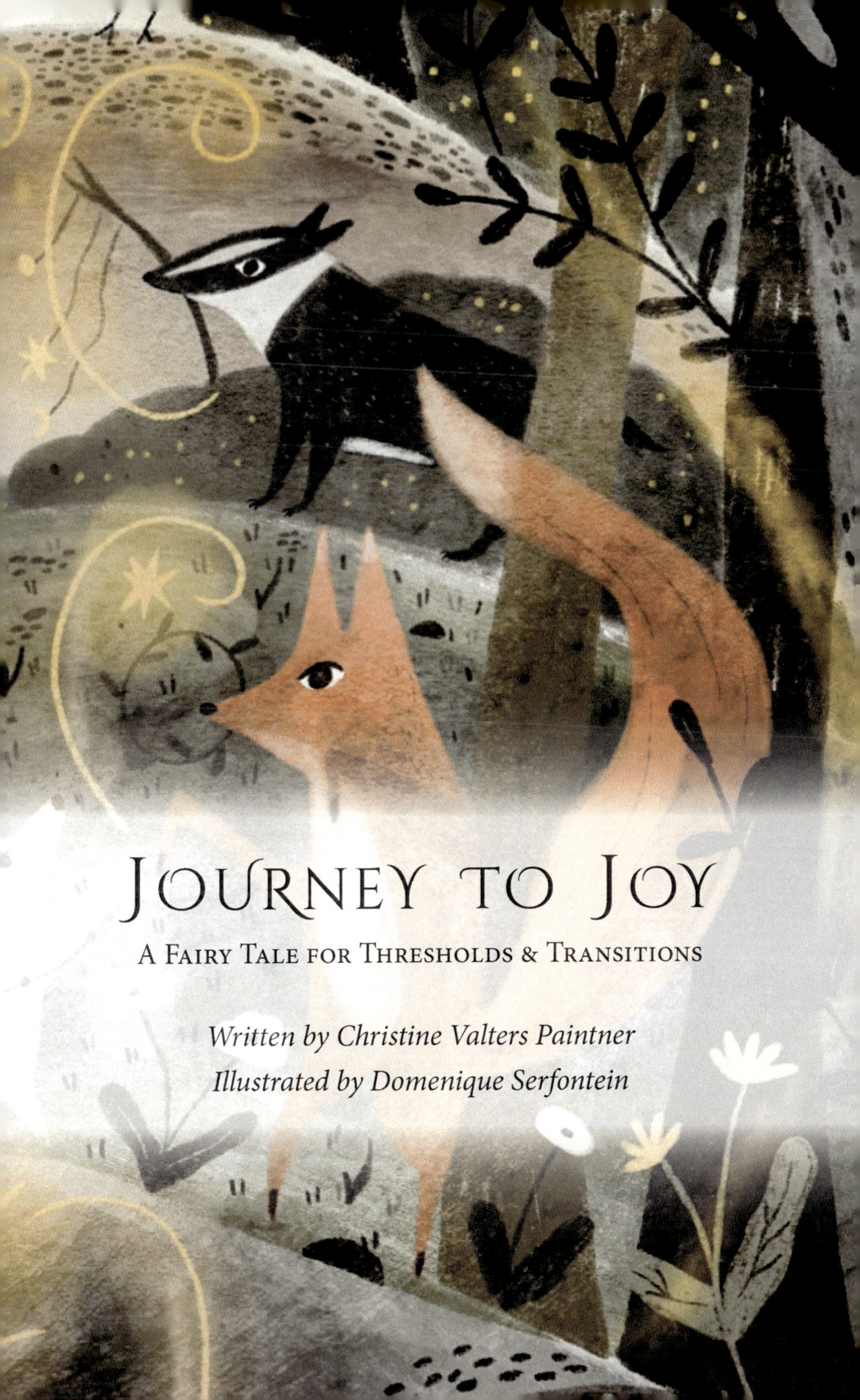

Journey to Joy

A Fairy Tale for Thresholds & Transitions

Written by Christine Valters Paintner
Illustrated by Domenique Serfontein

Print ISBN: 978-1-0683936-0-0

eBook ISBN: 978-1-0683936-1-7

To everyone who longs

to reclaim their full inheritance of joy

and who believes in the magic of stories

to transform hearts.

ONCE UPON A TIME THERE WAS A WOMAN IN midlife named Sophia. She lived in the village of Bad Freude[*] known far and wide for its healing springs that gushed up at the edge of the river and flowed along the town's border. Sophia worked as the village scribe, and it was her joy to spend her days writing poems and blessings to share with neighbors and other villagers. But, Sophia had not been well for some time and had to spend many hours resting in bed. With great devotion, she spent time watching the world, sometimes from bed and sometimes from her garden, and wove what she found there into words. These words gifted to others

* *Spring of Joy*

helped them slow down and see things more clearly. Writing helped her to hold the grief and joy of life together.

The village was also experiencing its own challenges. A long drought had slowed the waters of the healing springs to a trickle. The villagers were no longer able to take daily baths in those life-giving waters, as was their custom for generations. In addition, the steady flow of people who would come to visit to partake in the springs while staying in the various inns had slowed significantly. A sadness permeated the place. The villagers knew they had lost their spark but didn't know how to find it again.

Sophia rarely left the safety of the village as it had always held everything she needed. But one day, after several weeks of worsening symptoms and having exhausted her options for treatment in the village, Sophia decided to visit the Medicine Woman who lived on the other side of the river, far beyond the village edge. In previous years, anyone crossing the bridge to venture further to the woods or mountains beyond seemed to return more depleted than when they left. Still, Sophia felt this was her only option.

She packed her bag carefully as she didn't know how long she would be gone. Most importantly, she included her leather-bound journal and pen. She never left home without them. The dark brown leather, tooled by the village cobbler, was imprinted with a large S on the cover for Sophia. The paper inside was handmade by a local artist who kept Sophia in regular supply. The pen crafted out of oak by the village woodcutter fit perfectly in Sophia's hand.

Wandering along the cobblestone paths, Sophia's shoulders felt heavy and her back ached. Nevertheless, she stopped in various shops to say hello to friends and tell them where she was headed.

At the river marking the eastern edge of the village, she came to the Bridge to the Beyond. This bridge had a Troll secretly living under it whose

greatest delight was creating hardship for people. Every time someone crossed the bridge, the Troll would grow angry and would furtively steal their joy. Those who crossed were not aware and didn't understand why they always felt so tired when leaving the village.

Because of Sophia's weariness, she stumbled, and the Troll took advantage of the moment. Sophia blacked out briefly and when she awoke, unaware that the Troll was hidden in the darkness beneath the bridge, felt something drain from her.

Sophia continued on the path heading away from the village over what felt like an endless number of hills. When she came upon a stone to perch on or a tree to lean against, she paused to catch her breath or rest her aching feet. Sometimes she would eat an apple or some hazelnuts from her bag.

After arriving at the Medicine Woman's house, she realized she felt even worse than when she left her home and questioned her decision to make this journey. Her body slumped further, and her heart felt like a deflated balloon. The Medicine Woman had already prepared a pot of nettle and hawthorn tea, as well as delicious morsels of nuts and dried fruits, and greeted her warmly. She seated Sophia on a pile of soft blankets and furs and offered her warm lavender-infused water to wash and refresh herself.

Aware of the source of Sophia's worsened condition, once Sophia had rested and was refreshed,

the Medicine Woman told her, "When people cross the bridge, the Troll steals a bit of joy from them. She uses her cursed magic to put the joy into jars and then hides them in a cave deep in the woods protected by a dragon she bewitched and enslaved."

Sophia's eyes widened. "How do I retrieve my stolen joy?" she asked.

"The joy must be retrieved on the night of the full moon and the path to get to that part of the forest is swampy and dangerous. You will need to move slowly, despite your rush to retrieve what you are looking for," the Medicine Woman counseled.

Sophia rested a long while at the Medicine Woman's home to strengthen her body for the journey ahead. She drank teas and tinctures made for her from various leaves, flowers, and roots. She ate bowls of delicious stew and sat in the fragrant herb garden in between her times of rest, and her body slowly felt restored enough for more traveling. The Medicine Woman also reminded Sophia of her own healing power through the words she wrote and told her, "You will need this gift for the journey you will make."

Finally, after many days, the full moon rose round and white above the horizon and Sophia realized she had to go.

"But how will I find the Troll's secret cave?" Sophia asked the Medicine Woman.

"The cave is hidden deep in the forest, guarded by the Troll's dragon. Take Schatz[*] my Drachenhund.[†] She will be your companion and sniff out the dragon. There, you will find the cave."

* *Darling*
† *Dragon Hound*

The Medicine Woman packed her a satchel of supplies and sent Sophia on her way with her black, four-legged furry friend as a guide.

Schatz immediately darted to the north, and Sophia did her best to keep up. The forest was not very far, but as she got close, her feet began to slowly sink into the ground as she walked. Each step took enormous effort, and she moved more carefully to prevent getting pulled under. Lighter in size and four-footed, her small companion had an easier time crossing.

There were moments Sophia didn't think she would make it, but Schatz's wagging tail at the other end buoyed her determination. Sophia was already exhausted by the time she crossed, but as the moon rose higher, she knew she had to continue forward. Schatz ran excitedly ahead to show the way. Sophia could see her furry guide was not just leading her in the right direction, but also encouraging her to continue on.

Once at the edge of the woods, the tree roots offered them both more support. They walked among the oaks and pine, which grew ever thicker. On the rare occasions Sophia left the village, she had always felt at home in the woods, but this day she felt ill at ease knowing her task. She drew her cloak tightly around her.

The Drachenhund sniffed the air and started to whine. Her keen nose was picking up the scent of Dragon. In the distance, Sophia could see the cave. Outside was the shadow of the Dragon, large and dark. Schatz ran ahead to get closer and began to bark sharply. Sophia quieted her canine companion.

When she was a few feet away, Sophia could make out the Dragon's features and saw that he looked sad. He released a small flame from his nostrils to warn her against coming too close.

"Hello, Dragon," Sophia said. "Why do you look so forlorn when the cave you guard is full of joy?"

The Dragon sighed, "The Troll commands me

to keep people away from the Cave of Joy, but I too may never enter it and partake in its riches. I wish I didn't have to work for the Troll, she is a despicable creature." The Dragon lifted his back foot to reveal a magical chain that tethered him to a stone. "I am under the Troll's dreadful curse to protect this cave."

Sophia knew what she needed to do and pulled out her journal and pen. She wrote a blessing full of love to let the Dragon know she could see his true heart. Sophia began with, "I see you, Dragon, so full of beauty. You are a wondrous creation," and continued to invoke the words aloud until the spell came undone like the unraveling of a hundred knots. The chain dissolved into dust before them. With tears in his eyes, the Dragon blinked slowly in disbelief. No one had ever uttered words of love to him before.

Sophia asked, "Would it be okay if I approached and entered the cave?"

The Dragon nodded eagerly and stepped aside

to allow Sophia to enter the cave. It was dark and cool within its stone embrace. Heaps and heaps of jars filled with a golden, honey-like liquid were scattered along the cave's earthen floor. They held the joy of many of the villagers. She picked one up and tried to open it, but it was sealed too tightly. Then she tried another and another. Sophia felt despondent that she could not return with the jars to the village.

Though her shoulders slumped, she reached her hand out to the Dragon, beckoning him to enter as well. More tears rolled down the Dragon's scaly face as no one had ever before reached out to him and invited him to come closer.

He tried to open some of the jars with his great scaly hands but was also unable to do so. Sophia began to weep. She was so tired and did not know what to do.

The Dragon said, "There is a Wise One who lives just beyond the oak grove. They might be able to tell you what to do next."

“I don’t think I can go any further,” Sophia replied.

“I can carry you there,” said the Dragon. He placed Sophia and Schatz on his back, stretched out his wings, and flew beneath the full moon beyond the cave, above the thick canopy of oak trees, whose bare branches danced and glimmered in the moonlight.

THEY CAME TO A SMALL ROUND STONE COTTAGE with vines growing on all sides. A hearth fire was visible from the window even though it was now the middle of the night. The Dragon knocked on the door.

It creaked open revealing a figure with long white hair, bright green eyes, and a smile exposing several missing teeth. "I've been expecting you," the Wise One said. "Lay this Traveler down by the fire so she can rest a while."

The Dragon ducked to enter through the doorway. After nestling Sophia into a pile of blankets and pillows, he saw a table piled with food. While

Schatz's tail wagged vigorously, the Dragon's eyes grew wide and a bit of drool fell from the corner of his mouth. His cheeks flushed with embarrassment.

Realizing how hungry they must be, the Wise One said, "Help yourself and then get some rest. Tomorrow will be a long day. In fact, it will be a long year ahead."

The Dragon wondered what the Wise One meant by that but continued to eat and drink.

Sophia, already fast asleep by the fire, had strange dreams that night of unknown journeys to come.

When morning arrived, soft golden light spilled through the windows over the sink. The living room, dining area, and kitchen were all in one larger room, and then two smaller rooms on the side were for the Wise One's rest and one for their apothecary.

Sophia sat up slowly and rubbed her eyes. She gently stroked what she thought was a fur blanket on her lap, but then it stirred. When Schatz lifted her

nose into the air and leaned back against Sophia, the Wise One spoke.

"Now it is time to tell you what lies ahead." The Wise One poured a pot of tea made from dried rose petals and then served cakes infused with rose as well. The aromatics filled the room and made Sophia's heart quicken. She came to the table and held the warm cup in her hands, inhaling deeply. The Wise One continued, "With rose, we call in the sacred feminine, dear daughter. You will need Her wisdom." Sophia could feel an invisible mantle of protection surrounding her. It emboldened her for whatever might be ahead.

"I know you are here to retrieve your joy and bring joy back to your village. I know you want to be able to open the jars in the Cave of Joy. It is a noble task, but one that requires four initiations with the elemental spirits. Patience and endurance will be necessary."

The Wise One pointed to the white blossoms opening on the Blackthorn tree outside. "Spring is just emerging, and it is the time of the wind. When you feel ready, go outside and follow the breeze to the meadow of wildflowers. There you must find your song."

"How will I know I have found it?" Sophia asked.

"Everything in your being will tell you this is so." And with that, the Wise One stepped outside, and Sophia, knowing she was ready, followed. "Your friends can stay with me until you return as you have to make this journey on your own."

When Sophia journeyed to the cave the day before, it still felt so much like winter, cold and dark. But this morning, a blackbird was singing from one branch and a robin from another. The trees were budding, their vibrant green leaves ready to emerge.

Dandelions and clovers carpeted the ground.

A SOFT WIND WAS BLOWING, CARRYING THE scent of elderflower and lilac. Sophia inhaled again and smiled. Whatever was ahead, in this moment, she felt capable. She took her satchel, wrapped herself in her cloak, and followed the direction of the wind east beyond the cottage, through a cluster of hawthorn and hazel trees to a large meadow. The breeze invited her to the center of the meadow where she lay down on the soft grass. As she let her body soften to meet the ground, wildflowers emerged all around her. She could hear a humming sound and spent many hours and days listening to the songs of the various flowers until she could identify each one just by its melody. Weeks passed, and slowly she came to know the chorus of life all around her.

Sophia journaled many pages and sang songs her mother and grandmother had taught her, but she still wasn't sure what song was hers. So, she followed the wind to the mountain beyond. There she lay down on limestone and listened. Again, she spent days and weeks attuning to the song of the mountain, until she could feel it vibrating through her. Slow and deep, it was singing of ancient grief and endurance. Sophia could even hear the song of the fossils embedded in the ancient stone, and she knew that music was part of Earth's creation from its first forming.

Sophia still could not identify her own song, so she followed the wind once again to the top of the next mountain where she came across a plateau. She sat down and gazed out at the vista beyond. As day turned to night, the sky pulsed with a thousand

impossible lights. Sophia felt her breath catch as the pinpricked blackness erupted in a symphony around her. She could see the notes dancing in the light of the stars and in the empty voids between them. As she sat and listened, she could hear the music of the cosmos echo within her. The flowers and stone were still singing, joining in this harmony. Sophia knew music as primordial, and that she was crafted from these cosmic notes.

Sophia turned toward the canyon below and raised her voice into its great bowl. "What is my song?" she cried out. An echo returned with a question, and she could hear the voice of the wind.

"What is your truth?" it whispered.

Sophia felt her heart open and was overwhelmed by a tremendous love for all creation, greater than anything she had experienced before. She knew herself as intimately intertwined with everything. And Sophia began to sing, first a song of lament over the many great losses of her own life and those of her ancestors, then a song of celebration honoring the beauty of the world. Her voice carried her across the landscapes of grief and delight. She realized she was singing a blessing, and in the midst of her song she knew herself as a blessing in the world.

Sophia stumbled back with tears in her eyes. She bowed deeply to this plateau, this mountain, and the canyon beyond. Sophia went running back toward the Wise One's cottage to share her song with them. An entire season had passed since she left, and she was eager to see them all again.

The Wise One, the Dragon, and Schatz all awaited her return. They had prepared a beautiful meal and a resting place for her, and they could hear her song growing louder as she neared.

"You look different," said the Dragon when Sophia approached.

"Three months sleeping in meadows and on mountains will do that," she replied with a wink.

"Our Dragon friend can see how your song has filled you to overflowing. You carry yourself differently," the Wise One said. They put their hands on Sophia's shoulders. "You have done well, daughter. Now you are ready for what is next. Summer has come and with it the spirit of fire." They handed Sophia a candle and a scroll. "Tonight, once darkness descends, light your candle and let the flame guide you."

The Wise One brought Sophia tea made with angelica root. "To receive the protection and guidance of the angels," they said. Sophia ate and drank and slept. When the last glimmer of the sun had disappeared beneath the horizon, she brought her candle to the hearth, lit it, tucked the scroll into her satchel, and she began to walk.

SOPHIA WALKED FOR A LONG TIME, ALL THE while singing her song. The flame was guiding her south until she walked into a forest and arrived at a circle of trees; the candle began to dance. Sophia sat down on a large stone and opened the scroll, which had one sentence written on it: "Turn every burden you carry into lead and then walk through the flame."

Sophia felt a bit confused at first but closed her eyes to let the invitation wash over her and see what her intuition revealed. She remembered reading about the great alchemists long ago who would transform lead into gold. "How do I turn my burdens into lead?" she pleaded to the trees encircling her. "Bring them forth from you," she heard in response. She still wasn't entirely sure what this meant but knew her task was to listen to her heart.

Sophia spent the next several weeks pondering the burdens she carried, which she no longer needed to bear. Her parents died when she was young, and she had no siblings or children, so she often felt like she alone was responsible for everything. She worried about her health and for the rest of the village. Her journal was a vessel where she could write these burdens freely and writing helped her understand all she was carrying. She wrote furiously for hours and hours, pouring out her heart.

At night, Sophia would dream of all the expectations she had placed on herself and awaken in tears at the heaviness. Even though it was summer, and life was dancing all around her in vibrant hues, she felt grey and dark inside.

"How do I turn my burdens into lead?" she cried

out one morning after several weeks of pondering, tired of the weight of it all. She looked down and saw that a heavy leaden cage had formed around her torso. When she tried to get up, she strained to lift herself.

That night she built a fire as she did each evening. It took her much longer, caged as she was. But once the flames were burning bright, she knew she had to walk through them. Everything in her wanted to be free of these burdens. Sophia prayed to the angels and She Who Is for protection, so that she

would not be consumed by the flames.

Sophia stepped slowly into the fire; the heat was intense but did not scorch her skin. As she walked forward, dragging her heaviness, the lead of the cage turned bright yellow and began to melt away from her. The burdens were transmuted by the flame into gold. As the fire slowly receded, and the gold cooled, she bent down to pick it up and discovered it had taken the shape of a golden crown of branches. She placed the crown gently on her head and found the weight of her burdens gone. Her spine lifted; her shoulders broadened. Then Sophia lay down and fell into a deep and restful sleep.

The next morning, Sophia awakened to a pile of ashes left from the fire. She dipped her fingers into the ash and began to draw symbols of celebration and thanksgiving on her arms and legs, adorning herself with the power of burdens transmuted and summer's fullness. Then she walked back to the Wise One's cottage.

Sophia was quite a vision as she returned, gold crown shining, singing her song, her limbs coated with designs. Her hair was full of leaves and flowers.

Upon her return, The Wise One, the Dragon, and Schatz all welcomed her back with food and drink. Sophia feasted on the sweetest of summer's fruits and sighed contentedly with her fullness.

After another night of rest by the hearth, the Wise One awakened Sophia with a cup of elderflower tea. "Drink, daughter, and be nourished by the wisdom of the ancients. There are so many present here to guide you." Sophia received the scent, the warmth, and the sweet taste. When she closed her eyes, she could see a whole gathering of Wise Ones standing beyond the veil between worlds, raising their hands in blessing over her.

"What is next?" Sophia asked with some trepidation.

"Autumn is arriving and with it the spirit of water," the Wise One said. "You must head west to the Lake of Reflections. You will know what to do when you arrive."

SOPHIA HEADED OFF ONCE AGAIN, FOLLOWING the sun's descent. Six months had passed since she first arrived to the Wise One and Sophia was eager to be "ready" to retrieve her joy, whatever that might mean. Surely, she wondered, with her song in her heart and a crown of burdens transformed on her head, hadn't she done enough? As she walked among trees turning gold, russet, and ruby, she felt her heart grow lighter. She saw how everything was unfolding slowly around her. As leaves twirled to the ground, she saw the dance of release and decided to let go of the grumbling in her heart.

Just before the sun disappeared, Sophia saw it

ahead: a great wide lake. She went running toward it and fell to her knees at the water's edge. She saw her reflection in the still blue water. Her face peered back at her, the golden crown shimmering, and all around her own reflection were a variety of faces, all her own but with different expressions. Some looked sad, some angry, some confused, and some frightened. Sophia pulled back and inhaled sharply. Tears came to her eyes. She wanted to push the faces away, but the longer she looked, the more they continued to appear.

Sophia was exhausted and fell into a deep sleep at the edge of the lake. She dreamed of these parts of herself crying out for her attention: Grief, Anger, Melancholy, Confusion, Greed, and Fear—all with grotesque features. With long bony fingers, they all clawed at her at once, but she kept resisting and pulling away.

When Sophia awoke the next morning, she sat still for a long while and noticed that Fear was most present. Instead of pushing it away as she usually did, she straightened her crown and felt the presence of the Wise Ones supporting her. Her song arose in her heart, and she realized she needed a different approach.

Sophia turned toward Fear and spent several days listening to all this part of herself had to tell her. Fear told her many stories of wanting to protect her from various dangers.

As she listened, Sophia started to feel gratitude for the many ways this part of herself was trying to offer her a gift. She felt nothing but love, and in that loving gaze, Fear softened and shifted. They came to an understanding together about how to honor each other's needs.

After Sophia befriended and blessed Fear, Greed showed up for some attention. Sophia thought of all the times she hoarded things for her own benefit, and she recoiled at her selfishness. As she listened to Greed, she heard how this part had only wanted

to make sure she had enough to feel safe. She saw this gift that had been offered to her and started to feel love for this part as well. Greed then turned around, and Sophia saw the other side of its face was Generosity, and she breathed deeply, letting her heart expand.

Over the next many weeks, Sophia would awaken each morning and listen for which part wanted attention. Then, in the days that followed, she listened to, learned from, and eventually found she could bless and love that part. Through a long parade of old stories and new ones, she made peace with part after part, creating a loving partnership. On the other side of embracing Grief, she found the

face of Love, which revealed to her all the ways she had loved others and the world. Sophia saw how loss was a necessary aspect of Love, and she sat with that difficult truth for a long time. She embraced her Anger and on the other side found the face of Justice.

Sophia found a waterfall nearby with a clear green pool beneath it. In the afternoons, she stood under the rush of water, to feel herself refreshed and renewed, and then she would float. Each time, she could feel her body softening more and more. Sophia would spend hours here at the water's edge with her journal, writing love letters to the various parts of herself. She started to feel less divided and had more clarity about her life and her gifts and the

next steps after this journey.

Autumn was on its last release, the leaves had all made their descent to the soft earth, and one morning Sophia bent over the lake once again. To her surprise, this time she saw her own reflection, gold crown shining, and all the other faces were now a part of her. She had welcomed them back in with love and found wholeness within herself.

Then she saw something silver floating on the water in the center of her reflection. She reached down for it and realized it was a beautiful round pearl. Her eyes widened; her heart felt like it was rising in her chest. The water whispered to her, "You have transmuted your wounds into beauty, carry this gift with you as a reminder."

Sophia plucked it from the water and held the pearl in her hand, rubbing her fingers over its lustrous surface. It had a silver chain on it, so she could wear it around her neck like a talisman. Then she stood up, stretched her arms wide, grateful to this lake as teacher, ready to return to the cottage.

On her journey home, the air grew colder. The trees, which had dazzled her with their colors, now stood bare, skeletons against a steel sky.

When Sophia arrived, the Wise One, the Dragon, and Schatz all awaited her. The fire was ablaze in the hearth, and the table piled high with preserved fruits, honey, butter, and freshly baked bread. Sophia sat at the table and sighed with satisfaction. After filling up, she told stories from her time and read aloud poems she had written. Then she settled into the velvety pile of blankets and pillows, while Schatz nuzzled in on one side of her. She slept like that for three days.

On the third morning, the Wise One began to sing, summoning Sophia awake for the final of her four journeys. They handed Sophia a cup of tea. "Mugwort will bring forth healing dreams. Winter has come and with it the Dreamtime, daughter, and it is time to head north until you come to the Cave of the Ancestors. Listen to the spirit of the earth and you will find your way."

SOPHIA DRANK HER TEA BEFORE HEADING OUT. She walked under the sun low in the sky. She loved the long shadows cast in winter. It was beginning to snow, and she delighted in the flakes falling in a dance. She drew her cloak more tightly around herself.

Sophia sang her song, and even though winter was descending, she noticed that some of her energy was returning despite the cold. She touched the gold crown she was still wearing and thought of the inner communion of parts she had welcomed back. When she paused to rest, she reached to her neck to touch the pearl that had been gifted to her.

Evening arrived only a few hours later, and Sophia found herself at the mouth of a cave. She lit a candle and stepped inside where she found hundreds of skulls and other bones heaped along the walls. "The Cave of the Ancestors," she thought to herself. Intuitively, she knew these bones belonged to her and her people. In the center of the cave was a pile of blankets, and she lay down there, falling into a long sleep.

The first several days, Sophia dreamed of her mother and father. On the nights that followed, she dreamed of her grandparents. All of them spoke wisdom to her. When she fell into the dreams of her ancestors, dreaming of great suffering and times of famine, war, illness, oppression, and struggle, she could no longer tell which was her dream and which was theirs. She also dreamed of wondrous times of celebration—births and adventures, initiations completed, quiet moments of beauty, and many other jubilant times. For weeks, she felt herself woven into

this ancestral lineage of love as a thread in a tapestry.

One night Sister Death visited her dreams, and Sophia stirred as if from a nightmare but quickly fell back to sleep in the darkness of the cave. This happened for many days, until one night, remembering her experience at the Lake of Reflections, she decided to welcome her in. Sister Death pointed to all the skulls and told Sophia, "You will join these bones one day."

Sophia could feel this truth inside her. The longer they spoke, the more Sophia understood her mortality. She began to cherish the many quiet pleasures of her life. She fell even more in love with simple things like friendship and kindness and the way light spilled into her cottage back in the village on a spring morning. She knew Death would become her daily companion, reminding her of the goodness of living.

Sophia did not know how long she had been asleep, but when she finally awakened, there was a

single beam of sunlight penetrating into the cave. The bones were illuminated and it seemed as if they were glowing. She felt gratitude to her ancestors for all they had endured on her behalf and for all the dreams they had passed on to her. She knew herself as not alone in this world.

Sophia emerged from the cave to discover that spring had arrived once again in the landscape and colors were bursting forth everywhere. She gathered flowers, roots, and stones and brought them back to the cave where she created various pigments. She lovingly held each skull in her hand and painted leaves and flowers on them. She remained in the cave until she had painted and blessed each one.

After carefully placing each skull back where she'd found them, Sophia heard a voice behind her. She turned around to see a figure at the cave's entrance and drew closer. It was herself but older.

Her Future Self had grey hair tied back in a bun, a knowing smile across her wrinkled face, the same gold crown upon her head as Sophia's, and an entire string of silver pearls around her neck. "You now know yourself as woven into the past," her Future Self whispered. "I am here to remind you that you are woven into the future as well. These initiations will serve you well in the years to come."

Sophia and her Future Self began to sing their soul's song together, and tears ran down Sophia's face. This visitation from her future gave Sophia a vision of what might be possible and courage to keep going. Then, ready to depart, she stood and exited the cave, slowly walking away, back in the direction of the cottage.

When Sophia returned, the Dragon and Schatz were excited to see her. "Are we ready to retrieve the joy now?" the Dragon asked impatiently.

Sophia smiled and placed a hand on the Dragon; she invited him to sit with her and eat. Then she went to a quiet corner of the cottage to write about all that she had seen. Poems and blessings poured

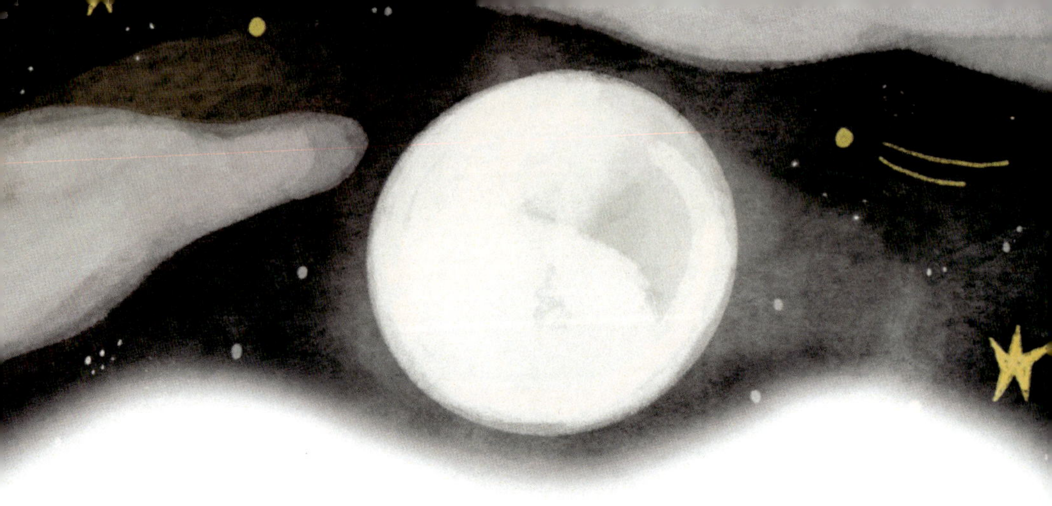

forth onto the pages.

"You have done very well, daughter. A year of initiation to ready you," said the Wise One. "You can now return to the jars in the Cave of Joy. You will know what to do."

Sophia's face crumpled at first. She'd hoped for clearer directions, but the Wise One handed her a cup of rosemary tea. "This is for remembrance. You have all that you need. May you remember who you are, who you belong to, and all you have learned." Sophia sipped gratefully.

"Tomorrow night, the moon will be full and you can head back then," said the Wise One.

So, they rested and waited until the sun started its descent. Then Sophia left the cottage again, this time with the Dragon and Schatz beside her. Under the glow of the rising moon, they headed back to the Cave of Joy, where she and the Dragon first met thirteen moons prior.

PUSHING ASIDE GOBS OF COBWEBS AND PILES OF mulch covering the cave's door, they entered and looked around at the mounds of jars. Sophia took one in her hands, the warm glow of it reflected off her face. She tried to open it, but nothing happened. She tried even harder, her skin turning red from her efforts.

The Dragon slumped and sighed, "Was all of that for nothing?"

Sophia stood, flooded with memories of the year that had passed: how her song wasn't just for her but to share with the world; how releasing her burdens had given her a new sense of her own power;

how befriending her inner parts kindled a deep compassion for herself and others; remembering how generosity lived on the other side of greed; and how the ancestors dreamed dreams that were not just for her own fulfillment, but in service to the entire community.

Sophia smiled and held one of the jars out to the Dragon. The Dragon's eyes widened, and he pulled back a little.

"What are you doing?" he asked. "You're the one who went on those journeys."

The wisdom Sophia had gleaned over her many initiations suddenly crystallized: "Joy shared is broken open and multiplied. This is for you."

Sophia extended the jar of joy across the space between them, and the Dragon reached out a scaly hand to receive it. He opened it effortlessly. Suddenly, he felt sweetness infusing his entire body, a sense of lightness and laughter permeated the air. Sophia's breath quickened with the magnificent radiance of

the golden light emanating from the joy as it shone throughout the cave. The Dragon turned and offered some to Schatz, and by now the joy was expanding exponentially. They all started laughing, deep belly laughs.

The Dragon sighed, "No wonder the Troll is so foul, trying to hoard joy rather than share it with others."

They heard sounds outside the cave and looked to find dozens of woodland creatures approaching. They were making music with pieces of wood and stone, acorns and seeds, and the birds were singing. All the animals were dancing. The joy's sweetness had spilled out beyond the cave's mouth into the forest drawing them all closer. Joy was irresistible.

Sophia, the Dragon, and Schatz joined in the dance, and all night they savored the delight of this communion of creatures. Fruits and nuts of the forest were piled high to feast on, and wine was made from berries to drink. They ate and danced until they eventually fell into a deep sleep, dreaming of laughter and promise.

The next morning, Sophia awoke feeling deeply rested, like her heart was going to burst. Joy had multiplied even further overnight, and she gathered it into her arms.

The Dragon woke with a big smile and told Sophia, "Now I want to serve joy and never again serve the bitterness of the Troll."

She embraced him and said, "Thank you, my friend, for all you are and will be."

With Sophia's hope restored, she danced her way back out of the forest with gratitude and delight. The Dragon and Schatz went with her, and together they carried the other jars they had found in the cave, now overflowing with joy, to return them to the villagers.

At the turn for the Medicine Woman's house, Sophia bent over to Schatz. She gave her a rub behind the ears, thanking this sweet being for guidance. And the Drachenhund scampered back home.

The villagers heard the Dragon and Sophia approaching town, and they all gathered on the far side of the bridge frightened of the large scaly being heading their way. Dragons were not usually a good sign, and Sophia had been gone for a very long time. But Sophia began singing her song and the villagers so delighted in the sound that they breathed a collective sigh knowing she was safe and well.

When the two came to the bridge, the Troll peered out from under it, but the Dragon breathed a

warning fireball in the Troll's direction so they could cross safely. Those whose joy had also been stolen embraced the Dragon as he returned what was rightfully theirs and soon the whole community was uplifted by the joy being shared.

At the same time, the healing springs began gushing with water again. Fountains erupted and pools formed for healing baths.

Sophia, now fortified again in body and spirit, lifted her hand to cast a spell on the Troll. She trusted the power and truth of her words. "For as long as your heart is a stone, your whole body will be as well," she uttered.

Suddenly, the Troll was changed into a statue, frozen in place, to give her time to reflect and learn. The villagers brought the statue out to the town square, so the Troll could witness all of their shared joy each day.

Sophia whispered in the Troll's ear, "If ever you desire to share in the joy yourself, you need only open your heart, and the spell will be reversed."

And so, the statue remains there in the village to this day as a reminder that joy shared can never be stolen. The time the Troll spent watching the world helped her to slow down and see the world more clearly, and maybe one day she too will let the joy into her heart and be transformed as well.

And Sophia, the Dragon, the villagers, and the freshly running springs lived joyfully ever after.

Let the joy in

QUESTIONS FOR REFLECTION

After reading the fairy tale through once or twice slowly, I invite you to spend some time in personal reflection. There are over 30 questions below. You might want to ponder one question a day and take a month or more to integrate the story's themes more deeply. Or you could look for the questions that spark something in your heart and spend time focusing on those.

With great devotion, she spent time watching the world, sometimes from bed and sometimes from her garden, and wove what she found there into words. These words gifted to others helped them slow down and see things more clearly.

> *What unique gifts flow innately from you? What gifts from others have helped you slow down and see more clearly?*

Writing helped her to hold the grief and joy of life together.

> *What does holding joy and grief together mean to you? Do you have practices that help you to hold the grief and joy of life together?*

The villagers knew they had lost their spark but didn't know how to find it again.

> *When was a time you personally lost your spark? Have you ever felt a communal loss of spark? How was that similar or dissimilar to a personal loss of spark?*

The paper inside was handmade by a local artist who kept Sophia in regular supply. The pen crafted out of oak by the village woodcutter fit perfectly in Sophia's hand.

What tools and supplies do you use that carry stories and connect you with a broader community around you? Consider how gratitude might be a path to forge a connection between you and your tools, regardless of origin.

Wandering along the cobblestone paths, Sophia's shoulders felt heavy and her back ached. Nevertheless, she stopped in various shops to say hello to friends and tell them where she was headed.

What is your current relationship to the concept of community? Do you experience it as a support system, a burden, something longed for, an ambiguous unknown?

Every time someone crossed the bridge, the Troll would grow angry and would furtively steal their joy. Those who crossed were not aware and didn't understand why they always felt so tired when leaving the village.

Do you experience your joy being stolen and drained by mysterious forces or metaphorical Trolls that you have yet been able to see, acknowledge, or name? What are ways you can attune your attention to notice when joy is being stolen?

After arriving at the Medicine Woman's house, she realized she felt even worse than when she left her home and questioned her decision to make this journey.

What are the journeys in your life you've questioned making after the initial experience didn't line up with expectations?

"How do I retrieve my stolen joy?"

Have you ever asked this question? Has it ever been answered?

"You will need to move slowly, despite your rush to retrieve what you are looking for," the Medicine Woman counseled.

Where in your life might you be advised to move slowly through a particularly dangerous landscape of your inner journey? What are some practices you could employ to remind yourself to move slowly and intentionally?

The Medicine Woman also reminded Sophia of her own healing power through the words [Sophia] wrote and told her, "You will need this gift [of writing] for the journey you will make."

Consider what healing power is intrinsic to your own being. What gifts can you offer both the world and yourself in the name of healing?

"There were moments Sophia didn't think she would make it, but Schatz's [Sophia's companion hound] wagging tail at the other end buoyed her determination.

What and who have buoyed your determination in the face of great obstacles and discouragement?

Sophia could see her furry guide was not just leading her in the right direction, but also encouraging her to continue on.

What guides have led you and also gifted you courage?

"Why do you look so forlorn when the cave you guard is full of joy?"

Have you ever felt compelled to guard your joy without feeling permission to enter fully into it? What were the forces or voices that forbade you entrance?

She wrote a blessing full of love to let the Dragon know she could see its true heart.

Have you ever gifted a blessing or received a blessing that dissolved joy-inhibiting chains? What is a blessing you could give yourself to begin to unravel the spell that keeps you from your joy?

Sophia began to weep. She was so tired and did not know what to do.

When your journey has left you weary and overwhelm clouds you, what are the ways you long to express yourself? Do you allow for these expressions of grief and disheartenment?

"I don't think I can go any further," Sophia replied. "I can carry you there," said the Dragon.

What is your relationship with help — both the offering and the accepting? What are ways you can embrace the blessing in both the giving and the receiving?

"With rose, we call in the sacred feminine, dear daughter. You will need Her wisdom." Sophia could feel an invisible mantle of protection surrounding her. It emboldened her for whatever might be ahead.

What symbols and traditions surround you and embolden you?

Whatever was ahead, in this moment, she felt capable.

Notice when you feel capable — in those times, what is it that surrounds you (physically, mentally, emotionally, spiritually) and calls for your attention?

She could hear a humming sound and spent many hours and days listening to the songs of the various flowers until she could identify each one just by its melody. Weeks passed, and slowly she came to know the chorus of life all around her.

When was the last time you slowed and listened so intently that life around you became as familiar as close friends? What has the world whispered to you?

Sophia knew music as primordial, and that she was crafted from these cosmic notes.

What elements of the cosmos have come together to create you? What pieces of the vast universe reverberate within you?

"What is my song?" she cried out. An echo returned with a question, and she could hear the voice of the wind. "What is your truth?" it whispered.

When at a loss of where to go or what to do next, have you ever considered posing your question to the universe? What question is longing to be voiced?

Her voice carried her across the landscapes of grief and delight. She realized she was singing a blessing, and in the midst of her song she knew herself as a blessing in the world.

What landscapes does your voice carry you across? What blessings within and around you are longing to to be named and sung?

"You look different," said the Dragon when Sophia approached. "Three months sleeping in meadows and on mountains will do that," she replied with a wink.

Though it may not be sleeping for 3 months among nature, what gifts of radical rest could you offer yourself? What are the effects of rest that you've witnessed in your life or others'?

Her journal was a vessel where she could write these burdens freely and writing helped her understand all she was carrying. She wrote furiously for hours and hours, pouring out her heart.

What vessel do you turn to in order to release your burdens and pour out your heart?

The burdens were transmuted by the flame into gold. As the fire slowly receded, and the gold cooled, she bent down to pick it up and discovered it had taken the shape of a golden crown of branches.

What burdens do you you carry that you long to be transmuted? Consider if there are past burdens that have already been transformed in some way.

"Be nourished by the wisdom of the ancients. There are so many present here to guide you."

> *Who do you turn to for wisdom and guidance? Are there ancient Wise Ones you feel connected with or invited to connect with?*

As leaves twirled to the ground, she saw the dance of release and decided to let go of the grumbling in her heart.

> *What in nature has presented you with symbolic invitations and lessons? What are ways you can practice making space and widening your attention to be more attuned and open to these invitations?*

She dreamed of these parts of herself crying out for her attention: Grief, Anger, Melancholy, Confusion, Greed, and Fear—all with grotesque features. With long bony fingers, they all clawed at her at once, but she kept resisting and pulling away.

> *What are the names of the parts of yourself that call for your attention? What do they look like, and what are their stories?*

Through a long parade of old stories and new ones, she made peace with part [of herself] after part, creating a loving partnership.

> *What kind of space would you need in order to listen to all the stories of all your different selves? What tools of compassion might help you begin to welcome all parts of yourself back home?*

For weeks, she felt herself woven into this ancestral lineage of love as a thread in a tapestry.

What is your relationship to your ancestral lineage? Deeply connected, fraught, cloaked in the unknown? What thoughts and feelings arise when you consider where you come from?

Sister Death pointed to all the skulls and told Sophia, "You will join these bones one day."

What experiences have served as reminders of your mortality? What has been your response to these reminders?

She knew Death would become her daily companion, reminding her of the goodness of living.

Right now, what is it that Death reminds you of? As you consider Sister Death as a companion, notice if anything shifts in the messages you receive from her.

"You now know yourself as woven into the past," her Future Self whispered. "I am here to remind you that you are woven into the future as well."

What are the ways you can acknowledge, honor, and embrace being a part of both the tapestry of the past and the tapestry of the future? What resonances and dissonances does this invitation evoke?

"You will know what to do." Sophia's face crumpled at first. She'd hoped for clearer directions.

In what area of your life do you long for clearer direction? What questions are you gripping in hopes of receiving an explicit answer?

"You have all that you need. May you remember who you are, who you belong to, and all you have learned."

> *When do you feel insufficient and incapable? What invitations of remembrance give you courage?*

The joy's sweetness had spilled out beyond the cave's mouth into the forest drawing them all closer. Joy was irresistible.

> *Reflect on a time when you experienced joy as irresistible. When has joy been a connecting force?*

"Now I want to serve joy."

> *What does "serving joy" mean to you? What would you change in your life in order to serve joy?*

"For as long as your heart is a stone, your whole body will be as well," she uttered. "If ever you desire to share in the joy yourself, you need only open your heart, and the spell will be reversed."

> *When has your heart been stone, closed off from joy? What have you discovered helps soften your heart to receive the gift of joy?*

Joy shared can never be stolen.

> *When and with whom do you share joy? How might you cultivate the reciprocal energy of shared joy?*

Acknowledgements

I am very grateful to my husband John who was so supportive when this story first emerged and gave me excellent suggestions for editing and crafting the story. He re-read it multiple times with each re-write and contributed a great deal to its final form.

Thanks to Carmen Acevedo Butcher, Aisling Richmond, and Polly Paton-Brown who read the story in advance and provided some wonderful and enthusiastic endorsements.

Much gratitude to Felicia Murrell, my excellent copyeditor and to Adam Thomas, my terrific book designer. I am so grateful to our wondrous program coordinator, Melinda Thomas, who has helped with getting this story ready and out into the world. And for admin team member Delaney Hart, who wrote the beautiful and provocative reflection questions at the end of this book.

And a deep bow of gratitude to illustrator Domenique Serfontein (*@maiden_moose*) who was amazing to work with. I received so much joy in writing the story which was then magnified with every illustration she sent to me. It is a wondrous thing to see a world you created take form visually.

Finally, to you dear reader, for trusting me with your attention and your heart. I hope this story has multiplied your own joy.

About the Author

Christine Valters Paintner, PhD, REACE, OblSB is the online Abbess of Abbey of the Arts, a virtual monastery and global community, where she leads online retreats, prayer services, and pilgrimages in joyful collaboration with many other artists and soul care practitioners. She is a poet and author of more than twenty books on contemplative practice and creative expression. Christine lives with her husband John and dog Sourney on the wild edges of Ireland in Galway City.

Abbey of the Arts

Transformative living through contemplative and expressive arts

We invite you to visit *AbbeyoftheArts.com* for more resources.

Made in the USA
Monee, IL
12 May 2025

04bbb100-feae-4ba7-90e6-a6a00daa13e0R01